THE ANIMAL

WILLIAM STAFFORD

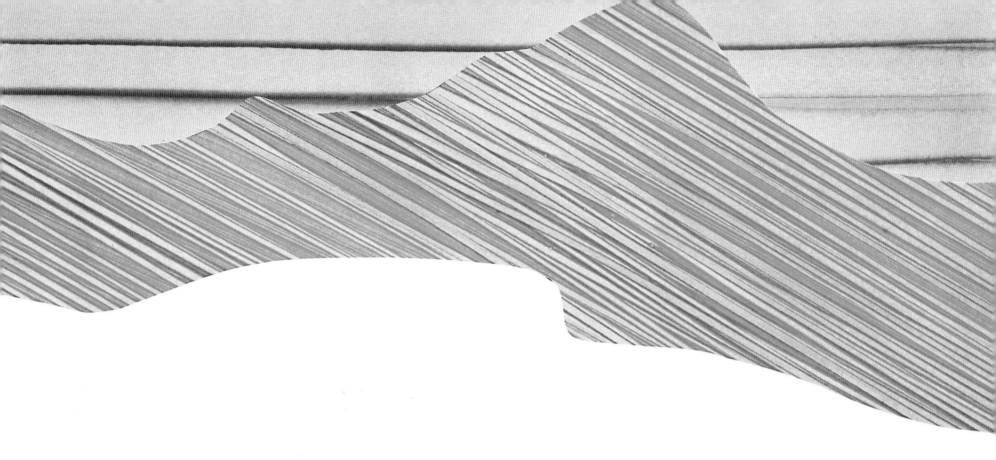

THAT DRANK UP SOUND

ILLUSTRATED BY DEBRA FRASIER

Harcourt Brace Jovanovich, Publishers

SAN DIEGO   NEW YORK   LONDON

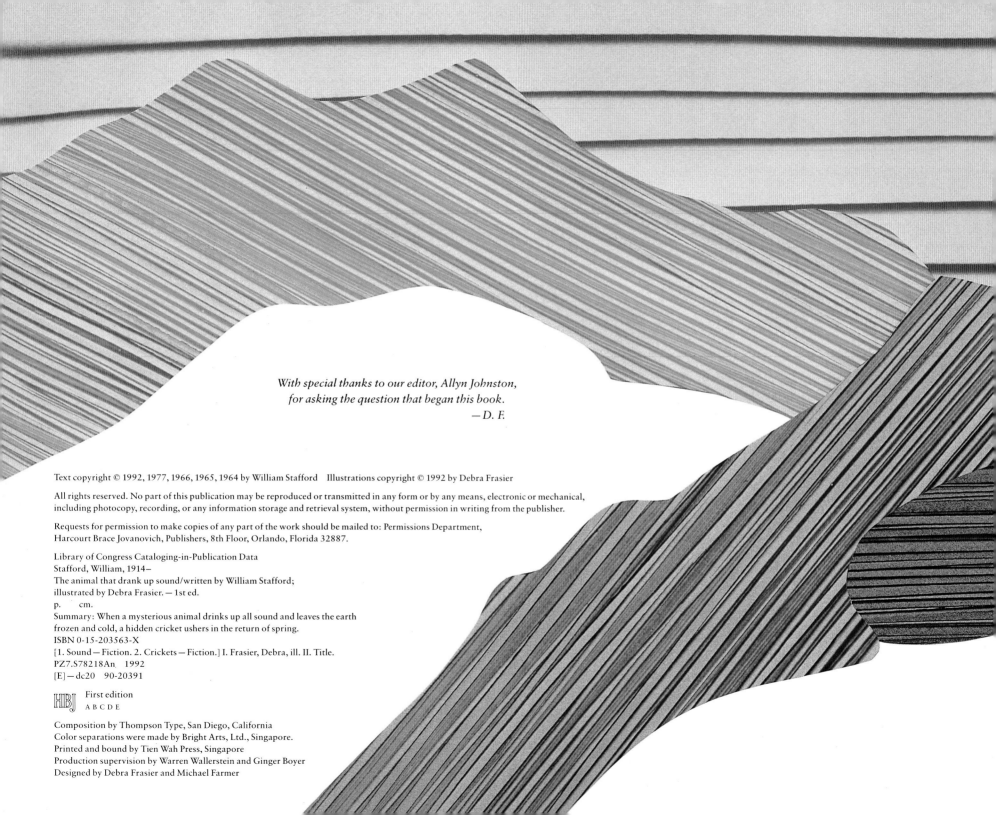

With special thanks to our editor, Allyn Johnston,
for asking the question that began this book.
— D. F.

Requests for permission to make copies of any part of the work should be mailed to: Permissions Department,
Harcourt Brace Jovanovich, Publishers, 8th Floor, Orlando, Florida 32887.

Library of Congress Cataloging-in-Publication Data
Stafford, William, 1914–
The animal that drank up sound/written by William Stafford;
illustrated by Debra Frasier. — 1st ed.
p.   cm.
Summary: When a mysterious animal drinks up all sound and leaves the earth
frozen and cold, a hidden cricket ushers in the return of spring.
ISBN 0-15-203563-X
[1. Sound — Fiction. 2. Crickets — Fiction.] I. Frasier, Debra, ill. II. Title.
PZ7.S78218An 1992
[E] — dc20   90-20391

HBJ   First edition
       A B C D E

Composition by Thompson Type, San Diego, California
Color separations were made by Bright Arts, Ltd., Singapore.
Printed and bound by Tien Wah Press, Singapore
Production supervision by Warren Wallerstein and Ginger Boyer
Designed by Debra Frasier and Michael Farmer

For our world,
where every color has a place and a secret reason . . .

— W. S.

. . . and for Jim,
who brought me to the edge of north, where color disappears.

— D. F.

One day across the lake where echoes come now
an animal that needed sound came down.

He gazed enormously, and instead of making any, he took
away from, sound: the lake and all the land went dumb.

A fish that jumped went back like a knife,
and the water died.

In all the wilderness around he drained
the rustle from the leaves into the mountainside
and folded a quilt over the rocks, getting ready
to store everything the place had known;

he buried — thousands of autumns deep —
the noise that used to come there.

Then that animal wandered on and began to drink
the sound out of all the valleys — the croak of toads,
and all the little shiny noise grass blades make.

He drank till winter, and then looked out one night at the stilled places guaranteed around by frozen peaks and held in the shallow pools of starlight.

It was finally tall and still, and he stopped on the highest ridge,
just where the cold sky fell away
like a perpetual curve,

and from there he walked on silently,

and began to starve.

When the moon drifted over that night the whole world lay
just like the moon, shining back that still
silver, and the moon saw its own animal dead
on the snow, its dark absorbent paws and quiet
muzzle and thick, velvet, deep fur.

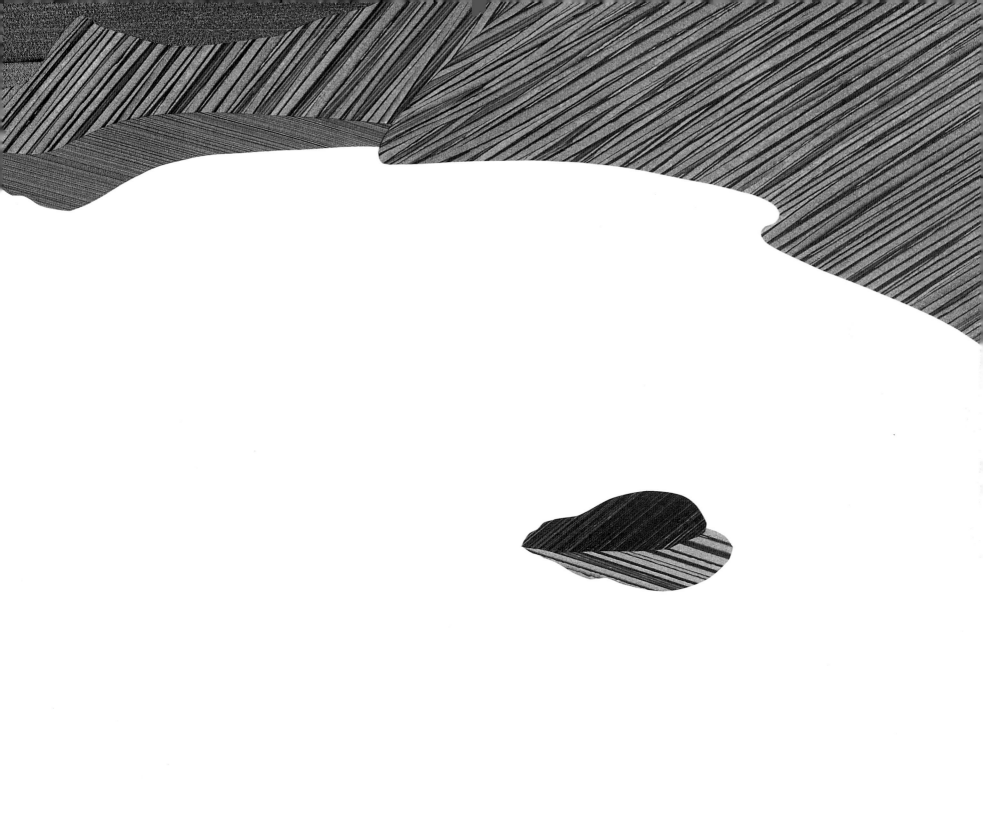

After the animal that drank sound died, the world
lay still and cold for months, and the moon yearned
and explored, letting its dead light float down
the west walls of canyons and then climb its delighted
soundless way up the east side.

The moon owned the earth its animal had faithfully explored.
The sun disregarded the life it used to warm.

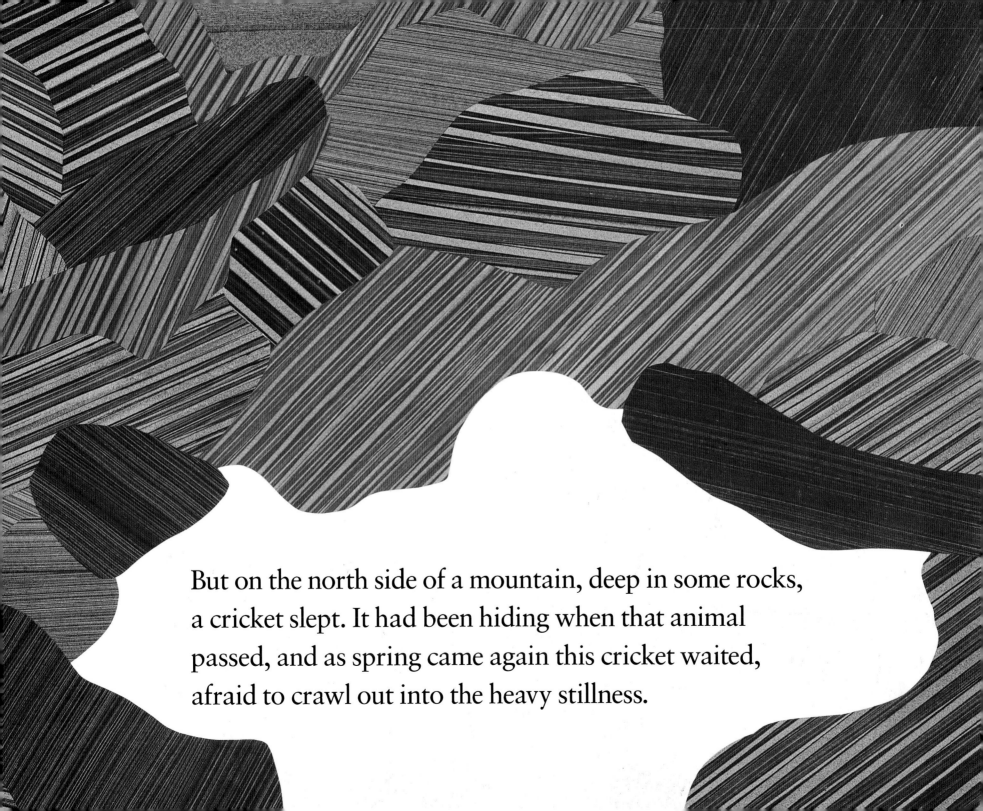

But on the north side of a mountain, deep in some rocks,
a cricket slept. It had been hiding when that animal
passed, and as spring came again this cricket waited,
afraid to crawl out into the heavy stillness.

Think how deep the cricket felt, lost there
in such a silence — the grass, the leaves, the water,

the stilled animals all depending on such a little thing.

But softly it tried — "Cricket!" — and back like a river
from that one act flowed the kind of world we know,

first whisperings, then moves in the grass and leaves;
the water splashed, and a big night bird screamed.

It all returned, our precious world with its life and sound,
where sometimes loud over the hill the moon,
wild again, looks for its animal to roam, still,
down out of the hills, any time.

But somewhere a cricket waits.

It listens now, and practices at night.

Notes from the Author and Illustrator

While our family circled a campfire by Devil's Lake in Oregon's Cascade Mountains, a friend told stories out of the dark, how everything was quiet and then a sound came nearer and nearer. The children drew together and leaned forward, and I wanted to have a story to tell.

From the lake we heard a splash — that's when it came to me, "The Animal That Drank Up Sound."

Once an idea like that begins, I urge it on, let it find words and big soft feet or whatever it needs. It can turn aside for a while and stop, then decide where to go next. If a lake is lapping, I let it in. If a night bird calls, I might even make it louder and more lonely. What the world gives me I welcome and weave it along toward the next thing.

If my story can find its way all over the wilderness and come home just right, then our family will always be together, by some campfire, leaning forward to listen.

WILLIAM STAFFORD

As the snow and bitter cold of my first January in Minnesota deepened, I brought "The Animal That Drank Up Sound" to the children I was teaching. Together we made masks for a performance of it, and through our dance I began to trust the promise inside this poem. Since that difficult winter I have grown to appreciate the hushed, stark beauty of this long season in the far north, but I still wait impatiently for one of the many things that have come to serve as my "cricket" — the first crocus tip pushing through wet snow or the first morning I can hear a drip falling from a high place. Transformation often begins with the voice of something tiny struggling to be heard, and this poem's assurance that crickets are hiding out there, waiting to usher in a warm change, is a great help to me.

I made the papers for these collages with a flour paste that is colored with acrylic paint. The paste is brushed thickly across wet paper and then wiped off in stripes, leaving a rich pattern. This paste paper is then dried on a clothesline and later ironed to flatten for cutting. The preliminary sketches for these collages were based on my visits to northern Minnesota, photographs of Yosemite National Park, and studies of polar and brown bears.

DEBRA FRASIER